THIS WALKER BOOK BELONGS TO:

_____

_____

_____

_____

To the Underwoods

First published 1989 by
Walker Books Ltd, 87 Vauxhall Walk
London SE11 5HJ

This edition published 1996

2 4 6 8 10 9 7 5 3 1

© 1989 Charlotte Voake

Printed in Hong Kong

British Library Cataloguing in Publication Data
A catalogue record for this book is available
from the British Library.

ISBN 0-7445-4791-1

Mrs Goose's Baby

Charlotte Voake

WALKER BOOKS
AND SUBSIDIARIES
LONDON • BOSTON • SYDNEY

One day Mrs Goose found an egg

and made a lovely nest to put it in.

Mrs Goose sat on the egg

to keep it safe and warm.

Soon the egg started to crack open.

The little bird inside was
pecking at the shell.

Mrs Goose's baby was very very small
and fluffy and yellow.

Mrs Goose took her baby out
to eat some grass.

But her baby didn't want to eat grass.
She ran off to look for
something different.

Mrs Goose took her naughty baby
to the pond.
The water looked cold and grey.

Poor Mrs Goose!
Her baby would not swim!

 The baby grew

and grew

and grew.

Mrs Goose's feathers
were smooth and white.

Mrs Goose's baby had
untidy brown feathers.

Mrs Goose had large webbed feet.
Her baby had little
pointed toes.

The baby followed Mrs Goose everywhere,
and cuddled up to her at night.

Mrs Goose guarded her baby
from strangers.

Mrs Goose's baby never did
eat much grass.

The baby never did go swimming
in the pond.

And everyone except Mrs Goose knew why.

Mrs Goose's baby was a

CHICKEN!

MORE WALKER PAPERBACKS
For You to Enjoy

Also by Charlotte Voake

FIRST THINGS FIRST
Shortlisted for the Smarties Book Prize

This baby's companion has everything from ABC and 123 to nursery rhymes, fruits and insects.
"Every page is a surprise... This really is the book to catch your child's attention." *Young Mother*

0-7445-4709-1   £4.99

TOM'S CAT

There are all sorts of noises around the house –
but which, if any, is coming from Tom's cat?

"Among my favourites ... ingenious and very funny."

Quentin Blake, The Independent

0-7445-1423-1   £4.50

AMY SAID
written by Martin Waddell

"A triumph… Text and pictures work in harness as the children provoke
one another to ever worsening behaviour. Understatement and lightness of touch
couldn't find better exposition." *The Times Educational Supplement*

0-7445-1779-6   £4.99

Walker Paperbacks are available from most booksellers, or by post from B.B.C.S., P.O. Box 941, Hull, North Humberside HU1 3YQ
24 hour telephone credit card line 01482 224626

To order, send: Title, author, ISBN number and price for each book ordered, your full name and address,
cheque or postal order payable to BBCS for the total amount and allow the following for postage and packing:
UK and BFPO: £1.00 for the first book, and 50p for each additional book to a maximum of £3.50.
Overseas and Eire: £2.00 for the first book, £1.00 for the second and 50p for each additional book.

Prices and availability are subject to change without notice.